The Evolution of Consciousness

ISBN: 9798334182509

The Evolution of Consciousness
By Maniyah Pulley

Direct author contact:
Maniyahpulley.poetry@gmail.com

For all of us that cannot put a period behind

“I am not alone”

Solus

- alone; separate

Before

Before is what we wish we were.

You can never go back to before.

Wishing to be indifferent to the world around you does nothing.

You will forever be in the present.

Never in the after,

Forever in the now,

Never in the past.

Before was better than now,

Better than the present,

More true than the future.

Being before consciousness is what we long for but,

Before is before.

That is it, that is all.

It is gone,

Never to return.

Concentrate

Humans are wonderful creatures,

Free to be who they are.

Free to experience the world in their own

Unique and special way.

Full of unknown details—-

Details that matter in the grand scheme

Of what this world must be.

Who are you?

You don't know?

Why not, how could you not?

You are you, aren't you?

Does the person next to you know who you are—

Who you are, truly?

Do you know if they know?

You don't know.

I wish I knew who I was—

Who I am.

Are you real?

Do you know?

Do you know if I am?

Please tell me you know..

Listen

The ocean waves crashing make a sound my ears long for.

The crickets make a bed of nails feel like a fluffy duvet.

The fly deafens a luxury.

Did you choose to not find the noise beautiful?

What is beautiful?

What could the definition possibly be?

Could you tell me?

You can't, and you never will.

I ask once again: who are you?

Quiet

I love the quiet,

the sound of nothing.

I'm not sure if I'm hearing “quiet”.

I was hearing quiet

Before I knew it was quiet.

I miss the true sound of nothing—

The true silence of an empty mind.

How does one know that sound?

Why do I love it?

Do others love it—

The sound of thoughts evading.

Do others love at all?

Thoughts

To have a thought is to...

To have a question means...

To be asking a question relies on...

To feel is to be human

I feel everything.

I feel the world around me,

Holding onto the questions I have,

Trying to gain the same clarity I hope to receive someday.

Do you feel it—

The lingering suspicion that you are not the only one with "..." at the end of your sentences.

Why can't you answer me?

Why can't I ask?

I

There is a "me."

There is an "I."

I must settle on some absolute truths.

What is absolute?

Can anything be absolute?

If not,

How dare I come up with such a word?

Do I have the power to do so?

Do you have the power to do so?

Who gave you this power?

Have you given it to yourself?

Have I given it to you?

Is there even power to be given?

Disdain

I don't like this.

I'm not fond of “why.”

I'm not fond of “who.”

I'm not fond of “how.”

I wish it were like before.

I want to go back to before,

Before consciousness.

Where I meant nothing,

Where words meant nothing,

Where we meant nothing.

Help

I am confused,

Confused with no one to help me bear the pain.

The pain of the unknown.

It hurts.

Everything carries pain.

The scrape of my knee may have hurt before,

But I did not remember the hurt.

I now remember the pain of memory

And everything that comes with it.

Do you?

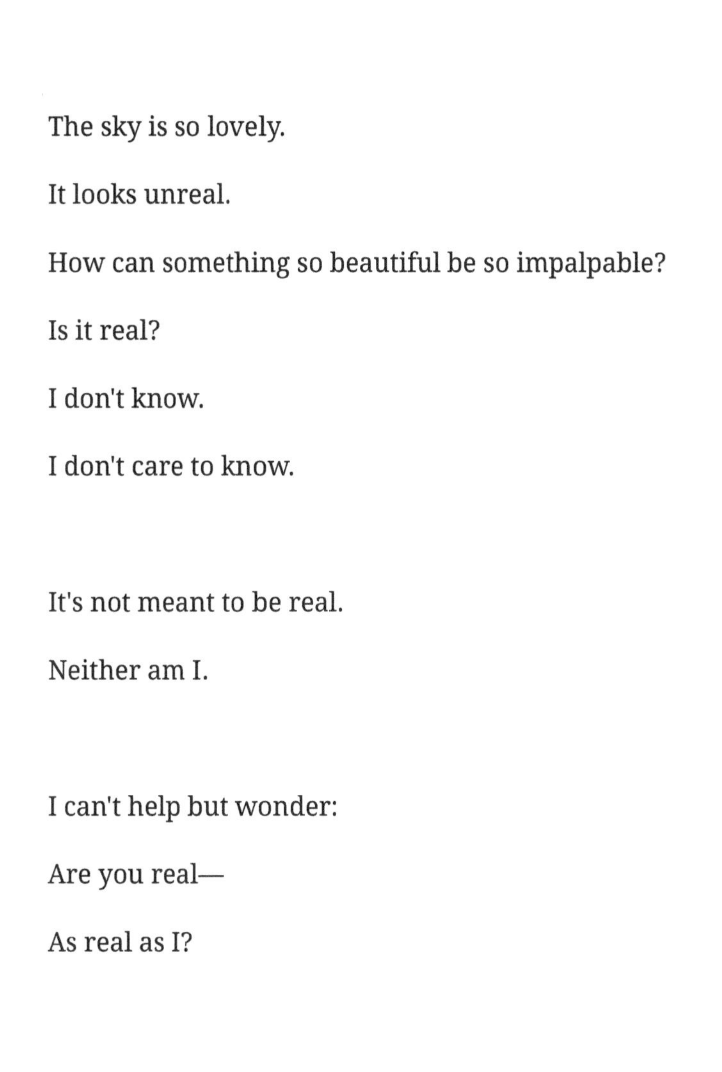

Matter

The sky is so lovely.

It looks unreal.

How can something so beautiful be so impalpable?

Is it real?

I don't know.

I don't care to know.

It's not meant to be real.

Neither am I.

I can't help but wonder:

Are you real—

As real as I?

Others

There are others,

More than just me.

There are other I's.

Maybe the others aren't I's.

Maybe the others are something beyond myself.

What if they are just like me, But not me?

Just hollow shells of what I think I am.

What if I am them, Not me?

What if there is no "me" or" I"?

What are we?

Look

There is a look behind their eyes,

A look of thinking, I assume.

When I look into the river on a sunny day, I see that look within me.

I am me because of the look.

I didn't have the ability to perceive this earth before,

But I know that before, this look in my eye was not there.

The look of thinking—

I see it in everyone.

I wonder if they see it in me.

Hello

As we gather the fruit from the bushes, I wonder if they are choosing for taste.

I cannot ask, So how will they tell me?

I have to know.

I choose the most delicious-looking strawberry there is.

I lift it to eye level to show them,

I wonder if they agree.

They add the strawberry to the basket. I wonder if they know why I chose it.

I wave to bring attention.

I now have it. How will I use it?

I taste the strawberry.

They taste it next.

They now know why I chose it.

They put the others back and now decide to start the picking with one that looks equally delicious.

Ants

We are together, Yet so separate,

Designed to think with no one to truly share it with.

We hunt, we gather, we eat—

Together,

Yet alone.

Building and creating, for what exactly?

Does it matter? Does it matter if it matters?

If I am not them, and they are not I,

We are different.

We think differently, we see differently,

But what are the differences exactly?

How do they come together as one?

We must have been doing this long before—

Long before consciousness.

Together

We are sitting in silence.

They signal me to follow them.

It's not gathering time.

We go to a tree, One that isn’t so interesting, at least not to me.

They stand still, staring at the branches and leaves.

But why?

They pick a leaf off the tree, one that has a hint of yellow.

They usually do this around this time.

There's a box with leaves, all brittle.

They add this leaf to the box.

We walk back in silence.

I don’t understand,

But in this confusion, I truly realize:

I am not alone.

Steps

I am free to do what I wish,

As I am not bound by primitive actions.

Maybe this will get me answers, But answers from whom?

Enough.

No thoughts; It's irrelevant.

If they can pick up leaves purely because they enjoy the color,

Then I can stop thinking purely because I enjoy the silence.

Taking a stroll through the trees reminds me of before,

Of what before must have been like.

No questions, no answers, Just being.

I miss just being.

I can't help but wonder:

Do they miss it too?

Feel

We sit on the grass with the others,

With the look of thinking in our eyes.

What are they thinking about? How will I ask?

Eye to eye: What are you thinking?

Darting back and forth, the thoughts are running rampant.

They grab my hand and pull me to my feet, taking me to the sunset.

It is so beautiful.

We sit and watch as the sun goes down.

I feel a peace in the silence. I think they feel the same.

Being understood.

We are thinking—

I am not alone.

Sonder

- The realization that each and every random passerby is living a life as vivid and complex as your own

What do you think

“Do you think about the sky?”

“It’s nice to look at, but not really. Do you?”

“Yes, it just seems so unreal.”

“How can it be unreal? It's right there. I see it, you see it, we all see it. It’s real.”

“I don’t think seeing something makes it real.”

“That’s illogical.”

“I know.”

Do you feel

“Do you know the feeling of a light breeze on a summer day?”

“Of course, it's so refreshing. Why do you ask?”

“I sometimes wonder if others feel things the way I do.”

“Probably not exactly, but similar.”

“How similar?”

“It ranges from person to person.”

“So, not similar to all?”

“Try not to think about it.”

“I’ll try.”

To prove is to

Stopping by the chain coffee store before work.

Printing out the latest email to keep record.

Taking care of those errands you were supposed to run yesterday.

Everyone has their own life to live.

Everyone has things to do, tasks to complete.

What if they don’t?

What if I'm just making it all up?

What if there are no other people?

What if it’s just me?

I can’t prove they feel what I feel—

I can’t prove they see what I see—

I can’t prove they hear what I hear—

I can’t prove they are like me.

What are you saying

“Follow me.”

“Okay. Where are we going?”

“Just trust me.”

“It's hard to do that when it's so late at night.”

“Come on. Would I ever hurt you?”

“Not to my knowledge, but hey, you never know.”

“Who do you trust?”

“Well, at some point you have to trust even when you don’t. So, I trust everyone, even if it’s not right now.”

“That sounds like a good pathway to insanity.”

My brain is me

I don't dictate much,

Nothing beyond my own personal actions.

Even then, I barely dictate those;

Outside factors are the main component.

This is true for many others,

Not all, but many.

My brain is in control.

It's hard being operated by something that isn’t me.

At least, it doesn’t feel like me.

My brain doesn’t understand.

I don't understand.

I say no

I don’t enjoy confusion.

I want to know the answers to my questions.

I want to know if people have the same questions.

I know they do,

There's no way they don’t.

I refuse to be alone in this confusion.

I am not my brain.

I am more than you,

I am more than me,

I am more than my thoughts.

I have to be.

Take the answer

"Why do you take this world so seriously?"

"Well, what else would I do? What else could I do?"

"Live with the impression that you don't matter and neither does anything or anyone else."

"That's very saddening and untrue."

"No. It's very saddening and most likely very true."

"Why do you have to take this world so seriously?"

"I am trying to find my purpose."

"Purpose isn't something you look for; it's something you stumble upon."

"Who told you that?"

"Myself. It's one of the many marvelous things my brain comes up with."

"You are your brain?"

"No, I am my soul."

I create my peace

What is a soul?

Where did people come up with this?

It cannot be real, as I cannot see it.

How dare I denounce such a thing?

Just because I cannot see it does not mean it is untrue.

But faith...

Such a strange thing.

No basis, but they choose to believe.

Why?

Fear, loneliness, grief...

Does it matter why?

It makes me feel warm.

I am choosing warmth.

I may not be my brain.

I may not be a soul.

But I am warm.

“That is enough.”

“You always talk to yourself in the mirror.”

“Of course, I’m the best person to talk to.”

“‘That is enough.’ What were you talking about?”

“I’m choosing to stop asking myself so many unnecessary questions.”

“Every question is necessary. How else would we know the things we know if no one asked?”

“I’m not sure, but that’s for everyone else to worry about.”

Just breathe

No more questions.

No more need for answers.

Just trust,

Just okay,

Just aware,

It doesn't matter.

A breath of fresh air—

What does that even mean?

All air is fresh, for the most part.

Sometimes we just want something different.
Sometimes we just don’t know how to say it.

I needed an anchor, something to pull me back to earth.

Something to allow me to live, Truly live,

Thrive even.

I want to feel alive, Not just be alive.

When will I understand

"How do you keep your faith?"

"I need it, the same as everyone else."

"I, too, enjoy the feeling of being looked after."

"We all do. Others just have a hard time admitting that."

"I don't see why."

"It turns their faith into something not larger than them."

"What's the problem with that?"

"When you are at your lowest, it takes your faith away."

"Not mine."
"Have you ever been at your lowest?"

"No."

"You will be, and you'll understand. Not everything is a matter of unanswered questions; some things are a matter of time."

"Not everyone gets time."
"That's why those who get it must appreciate it."

"But what about the questions that remain unanswered?"

"You must look at your past to find it. No question remains unanswered."

"That's illogical."

"Maybe, but it doesn't matter."

To accept is to

Walking alongside trees and grasses makes me feel alive.

Smelling the roses and lavender makes me feel alive.

I think more than anything, human connection makes me feel alive.

I love people and the things we do.

We take time to appreciate beauty,

In whatever form meets our wishes.

I like the choices we make,

Even the "bad" ones.

Bad choices make us human.

I like being human,

But I also like having something above this mortal form watch over me.

The feeling of being looked after by a perfect being can be compared to nothing.

I like that I feel.

I like that I'm not alone.

Authenticity

People pretend to enjoy solitude,

But I don’t believe we are wired to do so.

Those who pretend cannot cope with the fact that

They are not alone.

They never have been, and never will be.

Who is "I"

Why would anyone want to be alone?

I don't think anyone necessarily wants to be alone.

I think some find comfort in acceptance.

I find that I am one of those people.

I find comfort in understanding the way my brain works,

But I do not find comfort in seeing myself as just my brain.

What about when I die?

Where will "I" go?

I do not feel like I am my brain.

I am more than that.

Those watching over me have made me so.

Where will "I" go—

If I am a soul,

Where will I go?

What is the next step?

I need a destination.

Maybe that's what makes us human:

The desire for a destination.

Reask and reanswer

No questions,
No answers,

Just warmth.

But I like asking questions,

Even if I can never have the answers.

To me, questions must be asked.

Somewhere down the line, someone will answer.

What is wheat?
What is yeast?

What can we make using these things?

Someone had to wonder.
Someone had to ask.

One day, someone had the answer:
Bread.

Most importantly, someone again had to ask,

“What can we make with the materials given?”

Serendipity

"Hi."
"Hello."

"What are you doing out here at this time of night?"

"Why does it matter to you?"

"Well, I'm out here just enjoying the quiet.

Am I not allowed to know your reasoning?"

"I am doing the same, taking in the silence."

"What do you like about it?"
"What type of question is that? I, um, like the lack of sound. I don't know."

"I was just wondering if you appreciate it for the same reasons I do."

"Why do you appreciate it?"

"It can go away at any time, so I have to be grateful that it's here when I am."

"I think you just put my feelings into words."

"It's a gift."
"One that I won't take for granted."
"Good thing you're here when I am."

Purpose is the purpose

This world is a luxury.

Working together to build something better is a purpose—

Our purpose.

Do we work for the purpose, or because of the purpose?

I guess it doesn't matter because we feel fulfilled.

Funny.

The purpose is fulfillment.

I like that,

I like this,

Life.

A complete breath

All these people bundled up in a single lifetime—

In the grand scheme, we could have missed each other by just 100 years,

Never to know you,
Never to know who you truly are.

Will anyone be able to know who I truly am?

Will I ever be able to know?

On my deathbed, frantically searching for a memory to help,

Help understand why.

I enjoy the comfort of not knowing,

Not understanding,

For now.

But when it's my final breath,
I'd like to take it completely.

Indifference

- unimportance; little or no concern

A true love

Driving is peaceful.

Watching the trees go by brings me joy.

The scenery is incomparable.

Even traffic on a rainy night can bring a smile to my face.

Listening to each drop slam against my windshield is my flare at Point Nemo.

A rock dropping from the back of an old truck and leaving a crack—

laughter so big can arise from the back of my throat.

How could it not?

It's a proper ending to a dark night.

Someone sliding themselves in front of me when I'm almost late to work brings such a human feel to the world.

We are all doing the best we can with the little time we are given.

I love it, I love all of it.

I am chosen

My thoughts bring me a peace nothing else can.
Noticing the little things.

A tiny spricket found comfort in my basement.

Out of all the places it could be, it found shelter in my home.

It chose me—-

Something chose me.

I like feeling chosen, the same as many others.

I choose to find the small things that choose me beautiful.

It's only right.

So many beautiful things choose me every single day.

The leaves choose me to watch them fall.

The trees choose me to watch their branches grow day by day.

The flowers choose me to smell them.

They grant me a chance to make a wish.

Oh, how beautiful is life and everything within it.

I enjoy the choices I make

I am not the only one who has been chosen to experience the beauties of life.

We all are.

We have chosen people who will be in our lives.

Sometimes we don't get to choose, though,

and that's okay, because, in a way,

they have been chosen for us.

However or whomever may have done the choosing doesn't matter.

What matters is that choices make you who you are.

I choose to see the beauty in every choice.

Error

Work is draining some days:

making phone calls, answering emails, and going to meetings.

But that's okay.

I am choosing to have a place to rest my head after a long day.

I am choosing to open my fridge and have a meal awaiting my arrival.

I am choosing to go on a midnight shopping spree without worrying about the bills due at 12:01.

I am choosing to play the game.

Everything is a choice.

I am making the best ones—

at least the best ones I possibly can.

Continue to choose

I mean, look at how many choices one can make in a single day:

Choosing to wake up.

Choosing to brush your teeth, wash your face, get dressed.

Choosing to go to church on an early Sunday morning.

Choosing to go to work.

Choosing to take your kids to school.

Choosing to love your partner.

Choosing to continue to choose.

But how long can I make these choices before I start regretting them?

Making the “right” choice

I love life.
I love my choices.

I love when traffic slows me down.
I see the beauty in it.

I love having to pay for a broken windshield.
I choose to see the beauty in it.

I love working to barely afford my home.
I choose to see the beauty in it.

I am fulfilled.

I choose to see the purpose.
I can see the purpose.

There is a purpose.

There is a reason.
There has to be a reason.

I am choosing to continue despite not having a reason.

I’m choosing.

That’s all that matters.

I cannot continue

I'm breaking.

I don't want to make choices.

I can't understand why anyone would choose this.

I need help.

I need answers to the questions I don't have.

SOMEONE HELP ME.

“Please, I cannot continue to make these choices."

"Were you saying something?"

"Oh no, honey, I was just watching a show."

"Can you take me to a friend's house tomorrow?"

"Yeah, sure. What time?"

"12, tomorrow."

"Ok, I love you."
"Love you too."

Accepting the curse

Driving used to be my escape.

Now I am burdened by my thoughts, no matter how loud I play the music.

Lying to myself does no good either.

I am not happy.

I never really was, just short bursts.

So many people die when they don't want to,

but those that do are cursed with waking up another day.

I do appreciate the gift of life,
just for those that want to accept it.

But I haven't

For some reason, I feel that depression allows me to see so much.
I can see the trees.
I can see the sky.

I do find it and everyone beautiful
and worthy of life.

Just not myself.

It shouldn't be me.
God should have never chosen me.
Hell, what am I saying? There is no god.
There's nothing.
I have no idea why people even believe in such a being.

Any god of mine would have known that I would hate life.
To give it to me anyway is just some sick joke.

I have done EVERYTHING.

I have a job,
a home,
a family.

Everything that I'm supposed to have, I do.

WHY AM I NOT HAPPY?

We don’t matter

Maybe this is my punishment:

having everything I’m supposed to yet still being unhappy.

Maybe this is purgatory.

Let's not be ridiculous.

Humans don’t matter enough to get all the religious crap we think we’re going to get when we die.

WE GET NOTHING FOR OUR SUFFERING.

NOTHING.

NO MATTER WHAT YOU WANT TO BELIEVE, YOU ARE NOT SPECIAL.
YOU DO NOT MATTER.
YOU ARE NOTHING, JUST LIKE THE REST OF US.

It’s not about the truth

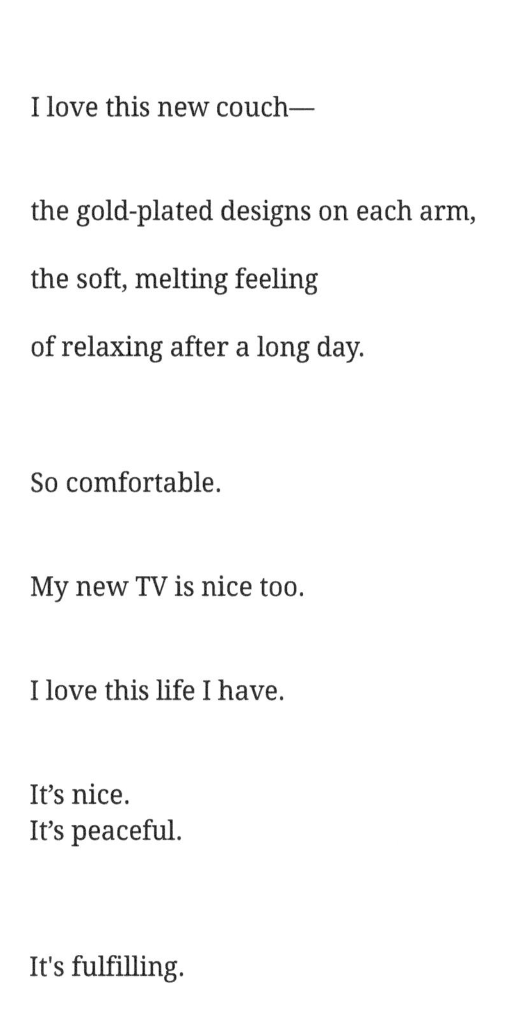

I love this new couch—

the gold-plated designs on each arm,

the soft, melting feeling

of relaxing after a long day.

So comfortable.

My new TV is nice too.

I love this life I have.

It’s nice.
It’s peaceful.

It's fulfilling.

Everything is fleeting

Why?

No, I'm refusing your answer.

I don't want to know.

I just want to be happy.

I just want to feel like my feet are on the ground.

I want to feel like I have a worthwhile goal—
something that isn't fleeting.

Everything is fleeting.

I hope I am alone—
alone in these thoughts.

But I'm not.

If I feel this way, others must as well,

as I am not unique or special.

No thought is original.

I am alone

“Hey, can I talk to you about something?”

“Sure, what is it?”

“I don’t feel happy. I feel like I’m waiting for death.”

“Well, everyone is technically. You don't have to just sit there and waste away. Do something you enjoy doing in the meantime.”

“I’m just tired of not having a purpose. Whenever I try to think of one, it just feels like a waste if I’m going to die anyway.”

“If you think like that, you’ll never be happy.”

“I know.”

Your choice to choose

I love music—
anything that has to do with art, really.

It's just not enough to keep me going anymore.
Nothing really is.

It doesn't matter, though.
I have obligations.

Choices to make.

I'm not alone in this.
Everyone has to make choices.

Most people don't enjoy it.
But hey,

the one constant in life is choosing.

Maybe I am

“Do you ever feel like your life isn’t what you expected it to be?”

“Yeah, all the time. Gotta keep pushing, though.”

“Yup, gotta keep pushing.”

Accedence

- To agree to a request or demand

I feel unwell, unnerved, and unwelcome.

Are these things I am or just things I feel?

I have so many questions with no answers to help.

As much as I try to stop for just a second, I can’t.

My life is tolerable.
I guess everyone's life is, if it wasn't, they’d end it.

Ending it is an option.
Not an option I want to take,
but an option nonetheless.

I don't care about the beauties of this world the way I used to.

I still care in a way, just not in the way I think I should.

The world is full of magical things.
We are one of them.

I don't think we were meant to exist.
I take that back.

We were meant to exist,
just not in the way I think we should.

Maybe we are the reason for our own demise.

I keep saying "we" when I mean "I."

I shouldn't put my thoughts onto you; it does no good for anyone, especially not me.

The life I have is worth living. I just can’t seem to understand why I don’t deem it worth it.

I understand there’s more to this world than my own opinions,
but I can't help but wonder if that matters.

Nothing really matters in the grand scheme.
Religion gives people the illusion they matter;
you don’t.

Spirituality and everything that has to do with it is beautiful, just untrue.

Trying to find comfort in it is fleeting.

When people realize it's simply for comfort, it takes away from the magic.

You're left with a turned stage and a glimpse of the beautiful woman hiding under the table.

Art is beautiful.

Discovering a new favorite song is something that keeps me going.

A lovely poem can keep me interested in life for just a little while longer.

Walking through a museum can amuse me with humans and the life we've created for ourselves, just a little while longer.

Art is what I feel we were meant for.

Creating is something we need to do to keep going long after we are gone.

I love it, I love us,
but I don't love this.

My favorite food is boring.
It’s still my favorite, though.

Work is dull, but it's tolerable.

Most things are dull but tolerable.

Why is everything dull?

Once again,
I’m asking questions I can never have the answer to.
I find beauty in it.

Not enough,
but some nonetheless.

I can't express myself in the way I'd like.

Something is holding me back.
I'm not sure if it's the languages we are bound by or if it's just me.

I know it's not just me, although I will never know the extent to which others think.

I'd like to think that we are all unique and original in thought.
I would also like to believe that we are all very similar in the way we approach our thoughts on life.

I am contradictory, but I like to think I am not alone in this.

The truth is, I am alone.

We are all alone.

Unable to allow everyone to see the "true" me.

~~My biggest fear is that there isn't a "true" me for others to see.~~

My biggest fear is perception.

Life is heavy.

It weighs so much on each and every one of us.
We are brought here and expected to achieve and succeed.

I am not built to achieve. I am built to exist.

Some of us were built to achieve.

Maybe it's just luck in the midst of existence.

It doesn’t matter, though.
No need to dwell.

No need to dwell on anything.

In a few generations, nothing I say or do will even be remembered.

Obsessed with the thought of just being.

Other animals just are.

At least as far as we know.

No limiting thoughts of death or what comes after.
It must be exhilarating.
Maybe not really, because you don't know what you have until it's gone.

Consciousness is a very funny thing.

You only know it because you have it.

You can't get rid of it.

You can only prove you have it.

I long for the ability to go back to before.
Before consciousness.
To just be who I am fully and authentically.

The thing is,
you can't go back,
and neither can I.

"I" is a concept created by our consciousness. I wonder if this is our way of putting meaning to something without it—life.

We give words meaning. Without us, there would be no meaning for meaning.

Purpose and fulfillment—
fleeting.

Even if I am alone in this, it doesn't matter.
Even if we are together in this, it doesn't matter.

Nothing really matters because we create meaning and everything within it.

I miss what it was like before consciousness, even if it takes consciousness to miss it.

I am choosing to go back.

I am choosing to appreciate what I had and who I met.

This was interesting, but I want to opt out of consciousness.

Religion is meaningless if I don't give it meaning.

Life is full of so many tremendous things—
just not enough to keep me going.

"What do you want to come from this?"

"I'm not sure if I want anything to come from this."

"Why?"

"Once again, another question I don't have the answer to."

"Why don't you wait and see if someone can answer it down the line?"

"I'm not interested in waiting."

"What are you interested in?"

"Stoicism."

"It's possible without the lack of consciousness."

"Maybe, but I'm not willing to find out."

"What are you willing to do?"

"Exist."

I am opting out
of the
human experience.

Epilogue

In writing this collection, I have stumbled upon questioning life in ways I hadn't before. I've always been intrigued by how early humans might have felt when consciousness was first thrust upon them. This awakening must have left them with questions about their own mortality, leading to conclusions that may be true or may not be. The questions they had and the questions we have today aren't very different.

Who are we? Why are we here? Why do we have the ability to perceive the earth in a way so different from other animals? These questions are painful to ask, and it hurts even more knowing that we most likely won't find the answers in this lifetime.

The statement, "I am opting out of human existence," reflects the choice of the "character" to end their life, seeing it as the only way to escape consciousness. We are not alone in asking these questions or reaching these conclusions. We share a unique type of loneliness, seeking others to share these questions with, or wondering if we should share them at all. You are not alone in this feeling.

We are all much more similar than you'd think. Just like people in 20 BC, we ask the same questions and often arrive at similar answers. They may have turned to religion or spirituality to cope, but some cannot find solace in either of those "solutions."

This poetry collection is a way to ask these questions and seek some form of an answer. It aims to convey a simple message: you are not alone in your longing for a simpler time.

— Maniyah

Made in United States
Troutdale, OR
08/08/2024

21868452R00054